HORTON and the KWUGGERBUG and More Lost Stories

TM & © Dr. Seuss Enterprises, L.P. 2014
All Rights Reserved

1 3 5 7 9 10 8 6 4 2

ISBN: 978-0-00-813127-2

Published by arrangement with Random House Inc., New York, USA. The stories and illustrations in this
collection were originally published separately in a slightly different form in *Redbook* magazine: "Horton
and the Kwuggerbug" in January 1951, "Marco Comes Late" in September 1950, "How Officer Pat Saved
the Whole Town" in October 1950, and "The Hoobub and the Grinch" in May 1955.

This edition published in the UK in 2016 by HarperCollins *Children's* Books,
a division of HarperCollins *Publishers* Ltd, 1 London Bridge Street, London SE1 9GF.

The HarperCollins website address is www.harpercollins.co.uk

Printed in China

HORTON and the KWUGGERBUG

and More Lost Stories

by Dr. Seuss

HarperCollins *Children's Books*

Contents

Horton and the Kwuggerbug

It happened last May, on a very nice day
While the Elephant Horton was walking, they say,
Just minding his business... just going his way...
When a Kwuggerbug dropped from a tree with a plunk
And landed on Horton the Elephant's trunk!

The Kwuggerbug leaned toward the elephant's ear.
"Perhaps you are wondering," he said, "why I'm here.
Well, I've got a secret!" he whispered. "I know
Of a Beezlenut tree where some Beezlenuts grow!"

Beezlenuts! Horton looked up with wide eyes.

Beezlenuts! THIS was a happy surprise!

For, of all of the nuts in that jungle to eat,

The nut of the Beezle, by far, was most sweet!

"But *why,*" Horton asked, "do you tell this to *me?*"

"Well, you see," the bug answered, "my Beezlenut tree

Is rather far off. And I'm not very strong.

I'd get there much quicker if *you* came along.

So I'll make you a deal that I think is quite fair...

You furnish the legs and you carry me there;

I'll furnish the brains, show the way to the tree.

Then half of the nuts are for *you*! Half for *me!*"

"A deal!" Horton said with a smile on his face.

"Hold tight and we're off to your Beezlenut place!

Just steer me and show me the best road to take..."

"No road," laughed the Kwuggerbug. "We'll take the lake!"

And he steered the big elephant down to the shore

Of a lake that was thirty miles long. Maybe more.

"Oh-oh!" shivered Horton. "Now wait just a minute.
I can't swim that lake. It has crocodiles in it!
Just look at their terrible teeth. How they flash!
They'll chew me right up into elephant hash!
I think, Mr Bug, that there surely must be
A *much* safer way to your Beezlenut tree."

"Now, now!" said the Kwuggerbug. "Don't start to squeal.
You promised you'd go. And a deal is a deal."
"Hmmm...," Horton thought. "What he says is quite true.
A deal *is* a deal. I must see the deal through."
So, bravely the elephant dived in that pond
And he swam and he swam for the shore far beyond
While crocodiles snapped and attempted to eat
His tail and his ears and the soles of his feet.
They nipped at his knees! And they nabbed at his chin!
And he thought, as he fought, that he never would win
But he swam and he swum and he held his trunk high
With the Kwuggerbug on it, quite safe and dry.
A terrible fellow! That Kwuggerbug guy
Just sat there and bossed him, "You hustle, now! Hustle!
I furnish the brains and you furnish the muscle!"

So, from ten in the morning till quarter past two
Poor Horton fought on till he finally got through
To the side of the lake where the Beezlenuts grew.
He crawled from the water, tired, battered and wet.
"Now *where*," Horton asked, "are those nuts that I get?"
"Oh," laughed the Kwuggerbug. "You're not there *yet*!

Climb *that*!" said the bug, pointing up in the sky
At a terrible mountain nine thousand feet high!

"Climb *THAT...*?" Horton gulped. "Not the way that *I* feel."
"Tut-tut!" said the bug. "Now a deal is a deal.
And don't start to argue. No *ifs* and no *buts.*
You'll furnish the ride and I'll furnish the nuts."

"The climb," sighed poor Horton, "will kill me, no doubt.
But a deal IS a deal, and I cannot back out."
He drew a deep breath and he threw back his shoulders
And dragged his tired legs over rocks and big boulders.
He stumbled and staggered uphill, over stones
That tattered his toenails and bruised all his bones
While the Kwuggerbug perched on his trunk all the time
And kept yelling, "Climb! You dumb elephant, climb!"
He climbed. He grew dizzy. His ankles grew numb.
But he climbed and he climbed and he clum and he clum.
His hearing grew faint. And his eyesight grew dim.
But he clum and he clum and he clim and he clim
From quarter past two until four-forty-five
Till, finally, old Horton, more dead than alive,
Had carried that bug to the very tip-top
And then, only then, did the elephant stop.
And he gasped to the bug, as he sank to his knees,
"Now where are my Beezlenuts, sir, if you please?"

"Right there!" said the bug. Horton looked. It was true.
'Twas the Beezlenut tree where the Beezlenuts grew!
"But, Bug!" Horton moaned. "We're *here* and they're *there*!
Way out on that peak, and between us is air!
Now *how* can I get through that space in between?
I can't walk on air, if you see what I mean!"

"A deal is a deal," snapped the bug. "I'm the boss.
You stretch out your trunk and you *put* me across!
Stretch, Horton! *STRUTCH!*" yelled the bug. So he strutch.
He strutch it two feet, but it *still* wouldn't touch.
"*Streech,* Horton! *STREECH!*" yelled the bug. So he streeched.
It hurt him real badly, but finally it reached.
"At last!" sang the Kwuggerbug, chuckling with glee,
And he slid down the trunk to his Beezlenut tree.

And he picked all those nuts and he stacked a big mound
Of luscious, sweet Beezlenuts high on the ground.
"But, hey!" called the elephant. "You! Over there!
Half of that mound, don't forget, is my share!"
"Not yet!" said the bug. "All the nuts have been stacked
But, before we can share, they have got to be cracked!"
So he cracked all the nuts. Then he said with a laugh,
"A deal is a deal, and I'm giving you half.
One half of each nut, as you know, is the meat.
And *that* is the half I am keeping to eat.
But half of each nut, as you know very well,
Is the half of the nut that is known as the shell.
The shells are for you!" laughed the bug. And he rose
And he stuffed all the shucks up the elephant's nose!

Now, what would YOU do
If he did that to YOU...?
With shucks up your nostrils, how dreadful you'd feel!
But you couldn't complain. 'Cause a deal is a deal.
You'd have to act terribly nice and do right
So you'd say in a voice that was very polite,
"Thanks, Mr Kwuggerbug! Thank you for these.
But they tickle my nose. *So look out! I shall sneeze!*"
And you'd sneeze and you'd sneeze!
And you'd snizz and you'd snizz!

And blow all the shucks from your trunk with a *WHIZZ,*
Just the way Horton did. 'Cause they blew out of *his*
And they blasted that Kwuggerbug *so* far away
That he sailed thru the air for the whole month of May
And didn't come down till the fifteenth of June,
All tattered and torn in the late afternoon,
At a place that's *SO* far, now he *never* can go
To his Beezlenut tree where his Beezlenuts grow.

Marco Comes Late

"Young man!" said Miss Block.

"It's eleven o'clock!

This school begins promptly at eight forty-five.

Why, *this* is a terrible time to arrive!

What's wrong with you, boy? Is your head made of wood?

Why didn't you come just as fast as you could?

What *IS* your excuse? It had better be good!"

Marco looked at the clock.

Then he looked at Miss Block.

"Excuse...?" Marco stuttered. "Er... well... well, you see,

Er... Well, it's like this... Something happened to me.

This morning, Miss Block, when I left home for school,
I hurried off early according to rule.
I said when I started at quarter past eight
I *must* not, I *will* not, I *shall* not be late!
I'll be the first pupil to be in my seat.
Then *Bang!* Something happened on Mulberry Street!

I heard a strange 'peep' and I took a quick look
And you know what I saw with the look that I took?
A bird laid an egg on my 'rithmetic book!

I couldn't believe it, Miss Block, but it's true!
I stopped and I didn't quite know what to do.
I didn't dare run and I didn't dare walk.
I didn't dare yell and I didn't dare talk.
I didn't dare sneeze and I didn't dare cough.
Because, if I did, I would knock the egg off.
So I stood there stock-still and it worried me pink.
Then my feet got quite tired and I sat down to think.

And while I was thinking down there on the ground,
I saw something move and I heard a loud sound
Of a worm who was having a fight with his wife.
The most terrible fight that I've heard in my life!
The worm, he was yelling, 'That boy should not wait!
He *must* not, he *dare* not, he *shall* not be late!
That boy ought to smash that egg off of his head.'
Then the wife of the worm shouted back – and *she* said,
'To break that dear egg would be terribly cruel.
An egg's more important than going to school.
That egg is that mother bird's pride and her joy.
If he smashes that egg, he's the world's meanest boy!'

And while the worms argued 'bout what I should do
A couple of big cats started arguing, too!
'You listen to me!' I heard one of them say.
'If this boy doesn't go on to school right away
Miss Block will be frightfully, horribly mad.
If the boy gets there late, she will punish the lad!'
Then the other cat snapped, 'I don't care if she does.
This boy must not move!' So I stayed where I was
With the egg on my head, and my heart full of fears
And the shouting of cats and of worms in my ears.

Then, while I lay wondering when all this would stop
The egg on my book burst apart with a *POP!*
And out of the pieces of red and white shell
Jumped a strange brand-new bird and he said with a yell,
'I thank you, young fellow, you've been simply great.
But, now that I'm hatched, you no longer need wait.
I'm sorry I kept you till 'leven o'clock.
It's really my fault. You tell *that* to Miss Block.
I wish you good luck and I bid you good day.'
That's what the bird said. Then he fluttered away.

And *then* I got here just as fast as I could
And that's my excuse and I think it's quite good."

Miss Block didn't speak for a moment or two.
Her eyes looked at Marco and looked him clean through.
Then she smiled. "That's a very good tale, if it's true.
Did *all* of those things *really* happen to you?"

"Er... well," answered Marco with sort of a squirm.
"Not *quite* all, I guess. But I *did* see a worm."

How Officer Pat Saved the Whole Town

The job of an Officer of the Police
Is watching for trouble and keeping the peace.
He has to be sharp and he has to be smart
And try to stop trouble before it can start.
And that's why, one morning, while out on his beat
On the corner of Chestnut and Mulberry Street
He got sort of worried, did Officer Pat,
When his very keen eyes spied a very small gnat
Going *BUZZ!* round the head of old Thomas, the cat.
"Aha!" murmured Pat. "I see trouble in *that*!"

If that gnat bites that cat, and he might very well,
That cat will wake up and he'll let out a yell.
That's only *small* trouble. I know it. But, brother,
One small bit of trouble will lead to another!

The trouble with trouble is... trouble will spread.
The yowl of that cat will wake Tom, Tim and Ted,
Those terrible triplets of Mrs McGown.
Then *they'll* yowl a yowl that'll wake this whole town.

When trouble gets started, it always starts more!
Those kids with their racket and ruckus and roar
Will frighten the birds, and the birds will come flapping
Down Mulberry Street with a yipping and yapping!

Once trouble gets going, it spreads just like fire!
Those birds will come screaming toward Mr McGuire,
The fish-market man. And he'll get such a scare
He'll toss that big codfish up high in the air!

That's the trouble with trouble.
    It grows and it grows.
That fish-in-the-air
    will land smack on the nose
Of that horse over there
    that belongs to Bill Hart.
The horse will start kicking
    Hart's wagon apart
And pumpkins will bounce
    on the head of Jake Warner,
Who's fixing that hydrant
    down there on the corner!
And once all those pumpkins
    start falling on Jake,
He'll fall on his wrench
    and the hydrant will break.
There's no stopping trouble,
    once trouble gets going.
When hydrants get broken,
    the water starts flowing!

The water will gush right on Mrs Minella.
She'll think that it's rain and put up her umbrella!
And *that'll* knock young Bobby Burke off his bike.
He'll fall on the ladder of House-Painter Mike!
And House-Painter Mike, when he tumbles, will spill
A bucket of paint on the head of Don Dill.
Oh, once it gets started, there's no stopping trouble!
That splashing of paint will upset Mrs Hubble.
She'll drop all her dishes. They'll smash on the ground
And startle her dog, and the poor frightened hound
Will jump in the horn of old Horn-Tooter Fritz...

And Fritz will fall backward and scare Driver Schmitz
On his Dynamite Truck almost out of his wits!
And that Dynamite Truck, with its big load of blitz,
Will race toward that tree and, oh boy! when it hits
The whole of this town will be blown to small bits!"

But lucky for us, down on Mulberry Street,
Good Officer Pat was awake on his beat.
And, quick, the brave officer swung his big bat
On the troublesome head of that troublesome gnat
And kept him from biting old Thomas, the cat,
And stopped all the trouble before it began.
He saved the whole town! What a very smart man!

The Hoobub and the Grinch

The Hoobub was lying outdoors in the sun,
The wonderful, wonderful, warm summer sun.
"There's *nothing*," he said, "quite as good as the sun!"
Then up walked a Grinch with a piece of green string.
"How much," asked the Grinch, "will you pay for this thing?

You sure ought to have it. You'll find it great fun.

And it's worth a lot more than that old-fashioned sun."

"Huh...?" asked the Hoobub. "Sounds silly to me.

Worth more than the sun...? Why, that surely can't be."

"But it *is*!" grinned the Grinch. "Let me give you the reasons.

The sun's only good in a couple short seasons.

For you'll have to admit that in winter and fall

The sun is quite weak. It is not strong at all.

But this wonderful piece of green string I have here

Is strong, my good friend, every month of the year!"

"Even so...," said the Hoobub, "I still sort of doubt..."

"But you *know*," yapped the Grinch, and he started to shout,

"That *sometimes* the sun doesn't even come out!

But this marvellous piece of green string, I declare,

Can come out of your pocket, if you keep it there,

Anytime, day or night! Anyplace! Anywhere!"

"Hmm...," said the Hoobub. "That *would* be quite handy..."

"This piece of green string," yelled the Grinch, "is a dandy!

That sun, let me tell you, is dangerous stuff!

It can freckle your face. It can make your skin rough.

When the sun gets too hot, it can broil you like fat!

But this piece of green string, sir, will NEVER do that!

THIS PIECE OF GREEN STRING IS COLOSSAL! IMMENSE!

AND, TO YOU...

WELL, I'LL SELL IT FOR NINETY-EIGHT CENTS!"

And the Hoobub... *he bought!*

(And I'm sorry to say

That Grinches sell Hoobubs such things every day.)